D0097583

Angel
Wings

For Amelia and Jemima King,

with love

First published in Great Britain in 2013 by Simon and Schuster UK Ltd
A CBS COMPANY

Designed by Amy Cooper

1 3 5 7 9 10 8 6 4 2

Simon & Schuster UK Ltd
1st Floor, 222 Gray's Inn Road
London
WC1X 8HB

Simon & Schuster Australia, Sydney

Simon & Schuster India, New Delhi

A CIP catalogue record for this book is available from the British Library.

PB ISBN: 978-0-85707-626-7
eBook ISBN: 978-1-47111-727-5

Printed and bound by CPI Group (UK) Ltd, Croydon, CR0 4YY
www.simonandschuster.co.uk
www.simonandschuster.com.au

Rainbows and Halos

MICHELLE MISRA

SIMON & SCHUSTER

Poppy
Ella
Tilly

Archangel Grace
Primrose
Jess

1 Brilliant Baking!

'Glittersome!' Ella Brown looked over Poppy's shoulder at the perfect heart-shaped cookies she was icing.

'Thanks, Ella!' Poppy pushed back her messy blonde curls. 'For once I've done something more neatly than you!' she teased.

As Ella looked down at her own cookies, she could see exactly what her friend meant. The icing was all wobbly, the shape looked more like a square than a heart and the cookies were all splodgy! Still, it was only their first angel baking lesson.

'I guess they don't need to look good to taste good,' Ella said hopefully.

'Well, we'll soon find out!' Poppy closed her eyes and took a bite of one her cookies. 'I wish for happy thoughts... ooh, that's lovely,' she smiled. 'Butterflies and bluebirds!'

Ella took a bite of one of hers. 'Ooh, yum,' she squealed as she munched. 'Delicious. It tastes of strawberries and cream!'

'Don't forget to make a wish before you finish it!' Poppy reminded her quickly.

Ella closed her eyes and thought her wish.

'What did you wish for?' asked Poppy

curiously.

'That it wasn't so hot!' sighed Ella. 'It's baking in here.'

Poppy nodded, fanning herself. 'I'm melting like an ice cream!'

'I've never known it be so sunny,' said Ella. It had been like this all summer term so far. They were in the middle of a heatwave at the Guardian Angel Academy.

'I hope the weather changes soon,' Poppy said. 'Or we'll be boiled alive at sports day next week! Imagine trying to run and jump and fly in this heat?'

Ella nodded and was just about to take another bite of her cookie when their form teacher came rushing over.

'Ella! What are you doing?' she cried out. 'Halos and wings! There'll be nothing left. We're

meant to be icing the cookies, not eating them!'

'Whoops, sorry Angel Seraphina,' Ella grinned. 'They are rather delicious though.'

'Oh, maybe I'll just try a little bit!' said Angel Seraphina. She took one of the cookies. 'Mmm, delicious indeed. Zero marks for neatness, Ella, but ten out of ten for taste!'

Ella glowed. She really liked her teacher.

Angel Seraphina turned to the rest of the class. 'Let's get tidied up!' she called out. 'The sooner we clear away, the sooner we can go outside and get some fresh air. Now, Poppy, can you bring your cookies into the other room. I want to have a proper look at them.'

Ella gazed out of the window to where a group of second years were playing angel volleyball. Multi-coloured butterflies swooped over the lawns and

the gentle hum of bees filled the air.

She turned and almost knocked over an angel hurrying past. 'Sorry, Tilly!' she gasped.

'No problem.' Tilly had light brown hair and was wearing a sapphire uniform. 'I'm just trying to catch ONE...OF...THESE...' The words came out in short bursts as she reached up to try and catch a chocolate cupcake that was whizzing above her head.

Ella fluttered her wings and rose up in the air, grabbing the cake. 'Gotcha!' She grinned. 'Here you go.' She handed it over to Tilly.

'Thanks, Ella!'

Jess, an angel with a long dark ponytail, joined them. 'Have you got them all?' she asked.

'Yes, Ella's just caught the last one.'

'Thanks, Ella,' Jess smiled. Tilly and Jess were the other two angels that made up a dorm with

Ella and Poppy. The four of them were the best of friends.

Ella looked at the flying cupcake in Tilly's hands. Its wings were beating frantically. 'Flying cupcakes are hard to make. You've done really well. My wish cookies are a mess. They don't even grant wishes,' she said looking out to where the sun was still beating down.

Tilly held the cupcake up to examine it. 'It was really all Jess's cooking not mine. But it does look good.'

'Let me see,' said Ella. She took it and her eyes glinted mischieviously. Angel Seraphina had gone through to the other cookery room with Poppy. 'Hey, it really flies well!' she said as she let it go. 'Look!'

It hovered above her head before shooting off and whizzing around the room.

'Ella!' Tilly and Jess exclaimed.

'Oh, no. We'll never catch it now!' said Tilly.

Ella giggled as Tilly flew into the air and chased after it. Every time she neared the cupcake, it jetted off in another direction, as if it was playing a game of tag with her!

Tilly finally managed to grab it. 'I'll get you for that, Ella Brown,' she called as she swooped down. 'Food fight!'

And, picking up the nearest spoon, she splattered Ella with some gloopy cake mixture.

'Right!' cried Ella, grinning, splattering Tilly in return.

'Stop it at once! You'll dirty my dress!' a voice behind them screeched.

Ella spun round. Primrose! She might have guessed! The most perfect-looking angel in the school was also the most odious. She looked Ella up and down with a snooty look. 'Haven't you forgotten the school rules? 'Angels should strive to be neat and tidy at all times."

Ella raised her eyebrows at Tilly and then splattered her friend again. Tilly ducked and it hit Jess head on.

'Ella!' Jess shrieked and then she burst out laughing.

'Well, I suppose that at least it wasn't my dress that was spoiled,' sniffed Primrose. 'Not that I'll be in this babyish white dress for much longer,' she said, doing a smug little twirl.

'Yes, we know,' Ella sighed crossly. 'You've only got one more halo stamp to get before you go up to sapphire level.'

All of the angels started in the first year at the Academy with plain white dresses and halos. As they did angelic things, they were awarded halo stamps and went up levels. White to sapphire, sapphire to ruby and so on, until they reached gold and then gold became diamond. That made you a Guardian Angel. Not only that but your wings grew at every stage until finally they were the largest, downiest of wings that changed with every colour of the rainbow.

'So how many halo stamps have you got left to get you to sapphire level, Ella?' Primrose asked, her eyebrows arched.

'You already know the answer to that,' said Ella with a scowl.

It was a bit of a sore subject. Whilst most of the first years had already got their sapphire halos, Ella still had to earn hers. Tilly and Jess had gone up a level last term and Poppy, like Primrose, was only one halo stamp away. Ella still had another three stamps to go. It seemed like a never-ending task!

Just then Angel Seraphina came back in with Poppy. They were both looking hot but Poppy was beaming. As Angel Seraphina fluttered off to help another one of the class, Ella went over to join her friend.

'You're looking happy, Pops.'

'I know!' said Poppy. 'That's because I am! I just got another halo stamp – for my cookies.'

'That's angel-tastic!' cried Ella. 'Doesn't that mean—'

'Yes! I've got enough halo stamps for sapphire!' Poppy exclaimed. Her excitement suddenly faded and she looked a little embarrassed. 'You don't mind, do you, Ella?'

'Mind? Of course I don't mind!' Ella gave her friend a big hug. Last term, she had been worried about how she would feel when the last of her friends filled in their card, so it was good to find that she actually felt all right about it.

'It'll be you next, Ella,' Poppy told her.

'I hope so,' sighed Ella, turning as a groan came from the other side of the kitchen.

It was Angel Seraphina, holding a sponge cake that she had just taken out of the oven. 'It's collapsed!' the teacher exclaimed.

Ella looked at the cake in Angel Seraphina's hands. The lovely yellow mixture had a big gaping hole in the middle of it.

'It must be the heat,' Angel Seraphina said. 'Well, that's it! I've had quite enough baking for one day! Come on everyone… outside!'

Ella and the other angels filed out of the kitchen and then flew down the corridor to the spiral staircase at the centre of the school. Stars and moons decorated the walls, and sparkly chandeliers hung from the ceiling. But despite it being beautiful not one of them wanted to stay inside that day. They swooped gratefully outside into the fresh air. It was lovely to be out of the hot kitchen and as they sped in and out of the shade of the trees playing tag, a gentle breeze rustled through the leaves. Ella sighed happily. She felt even better when she saw Angel Seraphina opening up a box of angel icicles!

'To quench your thirst and cool you all down,' Angel Seraphina called. 'One at a time, angels, one at a time and remember... they will taste of whatever you want them to taste of.'

'Lemon sherbet!' cried an angel, eating hers.

'This one tastes of cherry pop!'

'Blueberries and cream!'

Angel voices called out excitedly.

Angel Seraphina laughed. 'They give you happy thoughts too. Make the most of them, though, as we're running out and there won't be any more for a while.'

'Why's that?' asked Ella inquisitively as she took an icicle.

'Well,' Angel Seraphina looked worried. 'Unfortunately our water supply seems to be drying up. No one can explain it, but until it's sorted we just can't waste water and that means no more angel icicles…'

'Can't you use magic to make the water flow more strongly?' asked Tilly.

'It's a good suggestion, Tilly,' said Angel Seraphina. 'But we've tried that. In fact, we've tried just about everything that we can think of, but

nothing seems to be working. It's a real mystery as to why the water is flowing so slowly.'

Ella frowned. How strange. What would happen if it dried up completely? What would they drink? Or bathe in? And then there was sports day to think about too. They couldn't get through that without water. Not having enough water could turn out to be a real problem.

'Don't worry,' said Angel Seraphina, seeing the anxious looks on their faces. 'I'm sure we'll manage to figure out what's wrong soon and get it flowing again. Now, enjoy those icicles!'

☆ ☆ ☆

'Ella!' Tilly cried. 'Stop it, you're making me laugh!'

It was the next day and the first year angels were in their rainbow conjuring class. As Ella called out a spell, a spray of colours came flying out

of her wand, shooting up into the sky, then landing in the shape of a rainbow. Only this rainbow was square!

'Whoops!' Ella giggled. 'I'm useless at this rainbow conjuring thing.' She squinted her eyes in the bright sunlight, said the rainbow spell words and tried again. This time, a triangle-shaped rainbow appeared. She spluttered with laughter. The rainbows might not look quite right, but she was having a lot of fun all the same!

'I don't know why they're going wrong!' she said. 'It must be my wand.'

'Here, let me have a go,' said Jess, grabbing Ella's wand from her hand. She waved the wand and called out the rainbow conjuring spell:

Seven colours in the sky
Make a rainbow wide and high.

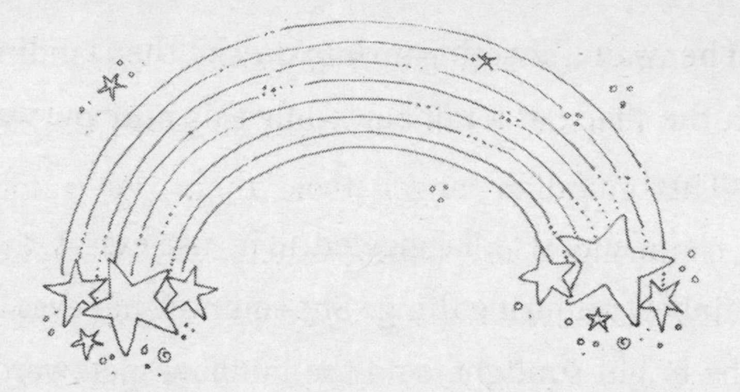

Seven rays of colour shot out of Ella's wand and made a perfect rainbow arching across the sky.

'Well, it's nothing to do with your wand,' puzzled Jess. 'It has to be something you're doing.'

'Oh well, who cares,' grinned Ella. 'It's fun!'

'Fun it may be,' a snooty voice came from behind them. 'But it's not going to earn you any halo stamps. Rainbows have to be perfect!'

'Hi, Primrose,' Ella sighed, rolling her eyes. 'Halo stamps seem to be all you ever think about these days!'

'Halo stamps? Who's thinking about halo

stamps?' a voice came from behind them.

Ella smiled at the sight of Angel Gabriella. The guardian angel took them for rainbow conjuring class, among others, and was one of Ella's favourite teachers. She was small and round with black eyes like currants, and reminded Ella of a bun. Her eyes were usually kind and twinkly but today she was clearly not going to stand for any nonsense.

'Come on, girls,' she said. 'You won't be getting any halo stamps if you just stand around talking. Making rainbows is an important part of being an angel. Go on, back to your own practising,' she said to Tilly and Jess. She looked at Ella's strange shaped rainbows. 'I think you need to practice too!' She pointed her wand at them and muttered a short spell. The rainbows dissolved into glitter and disappeared.

'Wow!' said Ella. 'How did you do that?'

Angel Gabriella smiled. 'With a little bit of advanced magic! Now I'm just going back inside to help out. We're having lunch outside today – a picnic – so practise a few more rainbow creations while I start getting it ready.'

'Do you need a hand, Angel Gabriella?' said Ella.

'Well, thank you, Ella,' Angel Gabriella smiled. 'That would be very kind. It was perfectly angelic of you to offer.'

'Angelic?' chorused Primrose, her ears pricking up. She hurried back over. Ella could tell she thought there might be a halo stamp on offer. 'I could help too, Angel Gabriella.' She fluttered her eyelashes. 'I'd love to!'

Angel Gabriella laughed. 'I think we'll be OK with one helper, Primrose, but thank you for

offering. Now Ella,' Angel Gabriella turned to her. 'Just practice a couple more rainbows, then come and meet me inside. And thank you again.'

'I promise I'll be with you soon!' Ella said. Her teacher hurried off through the heavy wooden doors that led into the school.

She was concentrating hard, conjuring her final rainbow, when Primrose came edging back over to her. 'Gosh, it's hot, isn't it?' she said fanning herself.

'Yes,' said Ella. She gave her a suspicious look. Primrose sounded remarkably normal and non-snooty. That was unusual enough. Ella couldn't help but feel wary.

'If only there was somewhere to cool ourselves down,' Primrose went on airily. 'Wouldn't that be wonderful? Somewhere where there was some cool, refreshing water to swim in. That would be

brilliant, don't you think, Ella?'

'Er, yes,' said Ella, wondering where this conversation was going exactly.

'Oh!' Primrose looked surprised as if she had suddenly thought of something. 'Silly me! Of course there *is* somewhere like that, isn't there? There's the Angel Fountain!'

'The fountain in Archangel Grace's garden?' Ella said. 'The one that is completely out of bounds?'

'Yes, that one,' said Primrose. 'Mmm, it would be so lovely to swim in that crystal clear, sparkling COOL water, wouldn't it?'

'I guess... if it wasn't out of bounds,' said Ella. She wiped her arm across her face. Talking about the fountain was making her feel very hot and bothered. It *would* be nice to have a swim in the fountain...

Ella quickly stopped herself. Whatever was she thinking of? Hadn't she learnt enough lessons in the past about doing things that she shouldn't? She'd got into trouble so many times before for breaking school rules. That was the reason she didn't have all her halo stamps!

Primrose hummed a little bit and bent down to the ground, picking a daisy. She turned it over and over in her hands. 'Of course, I can see why you won't do it. You're absolutely right to be scared, Ella,' she said, looking back over her shoulder and out of the corner of her eye.

'Scared?' said Ella in surprise. 'I'm not SCARED!'

'It's all right,' Primrose said sympathetically. 'You can admit it. Of course only someone super brave and daring would go into Archangel Grace's garden.'

Ella frowned.

'I wouldn't expect *you* to do something like that,' said Primrose lightly. 'Of course I wouldn't!'

And with a little smile she walked off.

Ella watched her go with her hands on her hips. What did the other angel mean exactly? Did Primrose think she wasn't very brave? Ella looked at her wand, then back at the small rainbow that was still hovering in front of her. The colours were all mixed up. She'd got the rainbow wrong... again. With one flick of her wand, the rainbow cascaded to the ground into a pile of heavy pieces. Not a piece of glitter in sight.

Ella hesitated. Angel Gabriella had said she should come in to help when she had finished, hadn't she? But maybe, just maybe, there was enough time to get to the fountain and back.

She thought of the tempting crystal clear

water. She thought about her friends' faces when she told them. She'd do it! What a story she'd have to tell them! She giggled to herself as she imagined how shocked they'd be. Ella fluttered the wings on her back and rose up off the ground. Checking there was no one watching, she swooped quickly away in the direction of Archangel Grace's garden.

3 Archangel Grace's Garden

The birds were singing in the trees and jewel-like dragonflies darting through the air as Ella came down to land in Archangel Grace's private circular garden. She sucked in her breath. It really was a magical place. Bright flowers filled the marble pots and tubs and giant butterflies

fluttered from flower to flower. There was a little gravel path leading back to the school and in the middle of the grass, stood the fountain – a white marble angel standing on a plinth, her wings outstretched as jets of water sprayed out from beneath her. At her feet, four dolphins spouted water that cascaded down into the crystal clear pool below.

Ella felt delight shiver through her. She couldn't wait to get in! She took a quick look around her. No one was about.

Quick as a flash, she took off her dress and fluttered up the side of the fountain in just her pants and vest. Then she dived in. SPLASH! The water was deliciously cool. She let her wings propel her forward like rockets. As the sunlight caught the droplets of water, she splashed about. This was angel-tastic!

She whizzed through the jets of water and then swam around in the water, ducking underneath and diving in from the side. She was having so much fun! The best! If only her friends were here to share it.

Her friends! Suddenly Ella stopped. They'd have finished practising their rainbows by now, wouldn't they? Suddenly, Ella was reminded of Angel Gabriella and her promise of helping with the picnic. She'd been much longer than she had intended. She had to get back!

She climbed out of the fountain and flew round it twice in the sun, her wings beating as she dried off.

'All done,' she giggled, quickly climbing back into her dress.

She was just about to head off when a noise stopped her in her tracks. Someone was coming

down the gravel path! There wasn't time to fly away. She'd just have to hide, and quick! Or she'd be caught.

Quickly, Ella looked about her. But where? She was running out of time. An angel came walking down the path, singing to herself – and it wasn't just any angel, it was a plump angel with enormous gossamer wings and dark hair coiled into a bun. Archangel Grace! The head of the school!

Quick! Ella jumped behind the nearest bush realising that the head teacher was dressed from head to toe in a striped bathing suit. She'd clearly had the same idea as Ella. As Archangel Grace climbed up onto the fountain and splashed herself in, Ella had to stifle a giggle.

'I'm forever blowing halos,' Archangel Grace's voice sung out as she floated on her back like a starfish.

It was just such a funny sight, Ella had to stifle her giggles. More pressing though, she was running out of time!

'Come on, Archangel Grace,' Ella muttered under her breath as the head teacher turned onto her tummy and was now doing a full lap!

Finally, just when Ella was about to give up on her ever getting out at all, Archangel Grace jumped out and started drying herself off in the sun.

Ella hesitated. Could she get across the grass without the head teacher noticing? It seemed unlikely. She would just have to wait.

And then, Archangel Grace pulled out her wand. What was she up to now? Before Ella knew it, the head teacher was calling out the rainbow spell and magicking up rainbows in the sky. They shot out of her wand in perfect arches and then, when she was happy with them, she would point

the wand and they would disappear again in a cloud of glitter.

Ella got a little closer. Archangel Grace's rainbows were the perfect shape and she loved the way they dissolved into glitter like Angel Gabriella's had. If only she could see what she was doing.

She heard the headteacher call out the spell to make the rainbows disappear:

Rainbow please, now vanish away
Turn to glitter, do not stay.

She flicked her wrist twice. Ella let out a little gasp as the spell worked and the rainbow turned to sparkling glitter. *I've got to try that when I get back!* she thought.

But first she had to get back. It seemed to take Archangel Grace forever to put away her wand and

start walking back up the path in the direction of the school.

Ella breathed a massive sigh of relief. At last!

Quick as a flash, she set off. Flying as quickly as she could, she rose up over the woods, heading for the school vegetable patch before coming back to land over by the trees. Only now, instead of a whole load of angels making rainbows, a big picnic was being laid out. Her class were there with Angel Gabriella, helping to put out the food and cushions.

'Ella Brown!' Angel Gabriella called out. 'Where have you been?' She looked stern as she carried a big jug of starfruit lemonade. 'I thought you were going to help me.'

'I... I can explain,' Ella started, and then she stopped. But she couldn't explain, could she? How could she tell Angel Gabriella that she hadn't helped her because she had flown to Archangel Grace's private garden for a swim?

'Yes, where were you, Ella?' Primrose had appeared behind Archangel Grace, carrying a plate of honey sandwiches. She looked pointedly at Ella. 'Luckily I was able to help Angel Gabriella. Where did you get to?'

Ella shot her a look. 'I was... I was...' Everyone waited for Ella to explain. 'I forgot,' she said finally, hanging her head to avoid seeing her friends' disappointed faces.

'Forgetting isn't good enough, Ella,' said Angel Gabriella sharply. 'You made a promise to help.'

'I know I did, Angel Gabriella,' said Ella. 'And I'm sorry. Truly sorry.'

Angel Gabriella hesitated but then her frown eased. 'All right. We'll say no more about it, but

I am disappointed. I'm going to have to de-award you two halo stamps. After all, a promise is a promise. Angels should never break their promises.'

Ella felt her eyes well up with tears and blinked them away. Two halo stamps! She knew it was fair, and that she only had herself to blame, but even so...

'OK,' said Angel Gabriella, clearly not wanting to press the situation. 'No harm was done,' she said breezily. 'After all, Primrose stepped in and was most helpful.'

Ella sucked in her breath.

'And for that,' Angel Gabriella smiled at Primrose. 'I'm going to award you a halo stamp, my dear.'

'Really? A whole halo stamp. For little me?' Primrose batted her eyes as if butter wouldn't melt.

'Thank you, Angel Gabriella.' Putting on a humble expression, she turned to face the other angels. 'My last halo stamp,' she said in triumph. 'I've filled in my card!'

Ella felt a lump in her throat. Not only had she gone and blown her best chance of getting a halo stamp but she'd gone and actually *lost* two stamps as well, *and* helped Primrose get to sapphire level at the same time!

'Well done, Primrose.'

'That's brilliant!'

Primrose's friends gushed as they gathered round to congratulate her. Primrose glanced back at Ella and gave her a sly smile.

Ella turned away. She couldn't bear to watch. How could she have been so stupid as to be taken in by Primrose? Was she ever going to get to sapphire halo level? If she kept losing halo stamps, she seriously doubted it!

4
A Big Problem

Ella's friends were despondent as they flew down the corridors and back to their dorm that afternoon.

'Oh Ella,' Poppy groaned as they pushed back

the door and flew inside. 'Whatever happened? You know how important it is for an angel to keep their promise.'

'I know,' said Ella, bowing her head as she jumped up onto the cloud that was floating around the room. 'I just forgot.' She felt terrible as she buried herself into her cloud bed. Hers was lilac, whilst Tilly's was aquamarine and Jess's was pale green. Poppy's was a pale pink. All that Ella wanted to do was hide under the duvet.

'So where did you get to anyway?' asked Tilly.

'You don't want to know,' Ella groaned.

'Try us,' said Jess, looking worried. 'Oh, Ella, what did you do?'

Ella gulped and told them everything – all about how hot she'd been and how Primrose had reminded her of the fountain. How inviting it had sounded, although she knew that it was out of

bounds. Before finishing on the fact that Primrose had said she wouldn't be brave enough to go.

'Oh Ella,' Tilly groaned. 'Couldn't you have guessed that it was a trap? You know what Primrose is like. You know she's always trying to get you into trouble!'

'I know, I know,' wailed Ella. 'I've only got myself to blame, but I just couldn't help myself.'

Jess and Poppy nodded. They knew what Ella was like too – knew how impetuous she was and how she loved a challenge.

'I feel so stupid,' said Ella, burying her face in her hands.

The other angels sat quietly.

'You could at least say something,' said Ella, looking up at them. 'Tell me that you would have done the same or something. Anything to make me feel better.'

The other angels looked from one to the other.

'Um...' Tilly said slowly.

'All right!' Ella burst out, tears stinging her eyes. 'So I'm stupid! The most stupid angel ever. I don't ever deserve to get to sapphire halo level. I get it!'

'Ella,' Tilly soothed. 'We didn't mean that. It's just—'

'Don't bother, Tilly,' Ella stormed.

'It's just that you were so nearly there,' said Jess. 'You only needed three more halo stamps.'

'Well, thanks for your support,' said Ella, jumping up off the bed and heading for the door.

'Ella.... Ella come back,' the angels called after her. 'But it was too late. Ella was off and there was nothing anyone could do to stop her...

☆ ☆ ☆

As Ella flew off down the corridors, her mind was in a whirl. She had to get away from there... away from all the 'I-told-you-so' voices. Quickly, she sped up until she reached the spiral staircase in the middle of the school and flew down it. Soon she was at the bottom. She pushed back the door and stepped outside. Although it was warm, the fresh air made her feel better and helped clear her head.

All Ella wanted was to be on her own, so she rose up into the air and flew off to the ornate greenhouses on the other side of the Angel Academy.

Gently, she came down to land and sat on the grass. She was so preoccupied that she didn't notice the little animal at first. As she buried her head in her hands, a little snuffly sound made her look up.

'Star!' she breathed. It was the little celestial hare she had looked after in the Spring term. He'd been released back into the wild but had made the woods around the school his home, so the angels often saw him. He particularly loved Ella because she had been the angel who had taken care of him the most. He stared at her. It was almost as though he had known that she needed him.

‘Come here, my lovely,’ Ella breathed, reaching out.

The little brown hare hopped towards her and brushed a whiskery face across her hand.

‘That tickles,’ Ella giggled as the hare jumped into her lap and snuggled up close. The little beat-beat of the hare’s chest pressed against her, making her instantly feel better.

‘Oh, Star,’ she sighed. ‘I’ve really messed up this time,’

She was just about to get up and let Star go when she heard a little noise behind her. Two angel teachers were coming down the path. She’d be in trouble for being outside so late if they saw her, and she was already in enough trouble today.

‘Shush, Star,’ she whispered. ‘They’ll never know I’m here, then I can go back inside after they've gone.' The hare twitched his nose as if he understood.

And so Star and Ella snuggled up tight and sat quietly. Ella realised it was Archangel Grace and Angel Seraphina.

'It is a worry...' came Archangel Grace's voice.

Ella listened in close. What could be a worry?

'Surely there must be something else we can try,' came Angel Seraphina's voice.

'But we've tried everything we can think of,' said Archangel Grace. 'The water supply is nearly dry.'

Of course! The water supply! With everything else that had been going on, Ella had completely forgotten about that. Now Angel Seraphina was starting to talk again.

'If we don't have enough water for people to drink and wash in,' she said. 'The school will have

to shut up early for the holidays.'

The school! Shut up early? Ella only just caught her gasp in time. But that would be terrible! They still had all sorts of fun things to do before the end of term – not least the school sports day and trying to get her halo stamps. No! School couldn't shut early! She needed to tell the others what she'd heard. Maybe they could all somehow help!

5 A Secret Surprise

With Ella away from the dorm, Jess, Tilly and Poppy had time to talk. They were all equally as worried about their friend.

'I just feel so bad,' said Tilly. 'It's not as though Ella forgot to help on purpose, and now she's further away from getting her sapphire halo than ever.'

'She needed us to support her,' said Poppy. 'Not have a go at her.'

'But how could she have been taken in by Primrose?' Tilly sighed. 'Again!'

'She just couldn't help herself,' said Poppy.

'You know what Ella's like. She can never stop herself. She's impetuous and brave and… and….'

'Kind and thoughtful too,' Tilly reminded them. 'Don't you remember that time she flew to Rainbow's End to get the forgetting flower for me?'

'And what about the time you all made that birthday glitter bomb?' said Jess. 'It was Ella's idea, wasn't it? OK, so it exploded when it shouldn't!'

'And she was the one who made sure Star was OK when Primrose was supposed to be looking after him but wasn't.'

The angels sighed. Ella was Ella.

'I feel bad,' said Tilly.

'I think we all do,' joined in Jess.

'We should try and think about something to take her mind off it,' said Tilly.

'What about a cake!' said Poppy. 'A totally brilliant cake – after all, we learned a lot in baking.'

‘That’s a brilliant idea, Poppy!’ said Tilly. ‘But it would need to be a really, really special one. One that could fly or grant wishes and taste really yummy too.’

‘All three things!’ squealed Tilly. ‘We should draw up a list of ingredients!’

'Do you think we can manage to make it?' said Jess.

'I don't see why not,' Poppy grinned. 'As long as you let me ice it!'

☆ ☆ ☆

'You're not going to believe what I've just heard!' Ella pushed back the door to the dorm. With a loud bang it sprang back, knocking the wall behind.

Tilly, Jess and Poppy nearly jumped out of their skins when Ella came in. They were sitting on Jess's cloud, a pad of paper open in front of them.

Tilly quickly closed it up and hid it behind her back.

'What's that, Tilly?' Ella looked at their guilty faces.

'Er... nothing, Ella,' said Tilly, turning red

and quickly flying down to her beside locker to put the pad away.

Ella bit her lip. They must have been talking about her and just didn't want to say. They'd probably been sighing over how stupid she was. She had just been starting to feel better too, after a little space and the fresh air had helped to clear her thoughts. Her friends looked at her awkwardly.

Ella broke the silence. 'Well... um, I came to tell you something,' she said, a little frostily. 'I just overheard Archangel Grace and Angel Seraphina talking. The water supply still isn't fixed. The school might have to closed early for the holidays!'

'But that's terrible,' exclaimed Jess.

'Oh no!' Poppy's blue eyes were wide. 'What will they do about sports day?'

'I guess it won't go ahead,' said Ella.

'But school can't shut early. There were so

many fun things planned,' said Tilly.

Ella swallowed. A lump swelled in her throat. It had been a long day. Suddenly she felt very tired. She didn't feel like talking anymore. She didn't know why, but for the first time ever at the Angel Academy, she felt like she was in it on her own.

Quietly she got undressed and into her pyjamas before climbing into her bed and pulling her duvet up to her nose.

'Are you OK, Ella?' Tilly asked.

Ella screwed up her eyes and didn't answer her. She bit down hard on her knuckles so they wouldn't hear she was crying.

'I think she could be asleep,' said Jess, after a moment.

Ella felt a wave of relief that they weren't going to ask her anything more.

Hugging her knees to her chest, she scrunched

herself up tight into an unhappy little ball.

☆ ☆ ☆

'One... two... three... take aim.' It was the next day and Angel Raffaella, the flying teacher, was taking them all for sports day practice.

A little niggling thought sat in Ella's head. *What would any of it matter if the sports day didn't go ahead anyway?* As Ella pulled back her golden bow, she squinted before taking aim at the heart-shaped target in front of her. The golden arrow raced through the air and then landed with a THWACK! on the outside of the golden archery board.

'Not bad, Ella,' encouraged Angel Raffaella.

Not bad, but not that good either. Ella sighed. She certainly wouldn't be earning extra halo stamps for her sporting talent that was for

sure. She was fairly useless at sports. But she still wanted sports day to go ahead. It would be fun just to be part of it and cheer everyone else on.

Ella looked across the field to where the other angels were practicing the different events. A group of angels were over by the school vegetable patch doing halo hoopla, whilst another group were by the trees throwing the rainbow discus, all closely supervised by Angel Raffaella.

Ella, Tilly and Jess were in silver sacks, practising for the sack race. Ella bit her lip. They'd asked her to join in with them but she'd refused. They'd all been whispering again over breakfast and she wanted to show them she didn't care. But now as she looked across the field, she could see they were having a whole heap of fun and she wished she hadn't been so stubborn. Taking a deep breath, she decided to go over.

As she went over they all sprawled across the finish line, falling over on top of each other. They lay there laughing.

'Hi!' Ella tried to sound breezy. 'How's it going?'

'Er... good, Ella,' said Jess. 'Look, we didn't mean anything earlier when we were talking at breakfast,' she said. 'Honestly we didn't.'

'It doesn't matter,' said Ella, trying to look nonchalant. 'I just thought I'd come and see how you were getting on. There's extra flying practice after sports for anyone who wants to go along,' she said, offering an olive branch. 'To practise for the three-winged race. Does anyone want to come with me?'

'Er, that sounds good, but I can't,' said Jess.

Ella couldn't help but notice Jess fling a look at Tilly.

'What about you, Tilly?' said Ella.

'Er, I'm kind of busy,' said Tilly.

'And you?' Ella turned to Poppy.

Poppy turned bright red. 'I've got something on too.'

That was it! It was too much for Ella. Something was definitely going on with her friends. 'Fine,' she mumbled, turning on her heels, tears prickling her eyes. 'I'll just go on my own then.'

'Ella,' Poppy cried out.

But Ella was already off, hurrying across the field...

6
Out of Bounds

Ella flew into the sky. She knew she shouldn't but she just didn't want to be around anyone. She could hear her friends calling out after her, but she didn't stop. It was the end of the lesson now anyway and she didn't feel like joining the

three-winged flying practice after all – not if she was going to be doing it by herself. She'd just go for a fly to get away from everything.

Ella rose up high in the sky, beating her wings as fast as they would go. As the air rushed past her, she began to feel better. Soon she was so high that the glass castle of the Angel Academy below her was just a pinprick, sparkling like a diamond in the sunshine.

Seeing it at such a distance made her unhappiness fade. What went on at school suddenly didn't seem to matter. She looped-the-loop and found herself laughing. A group of friendly skylarks swooped towards her and she flew with them, surrounded by their fluttering wings.

'See you later,' she called to the birds as they flew on.

She looked down. She was flying over the river that brought the water to the school. Bluebell Woods lay in her sights, small blue flowers carpeting the ground beneath the trees. She started to feel a little concerned. She'd actually flown rather a long way from school. First year angels weren't allowed to fly beyond the school boundaries without permission. She groaned. She was going to be in big trouble AGAIN if she didn't get back before any of the teachers noticed she was gone. Oh why did she always get herself into these scrapes?

Ella turned back to the school but as she did so, her eyes caught sight of something beneath her. The river was a sparkling blue in the sunshine but there was something bright and colourful lying across it – blocking it like a dam.

Ella squinted in the sunlight, and sucked in

her breath as she realised what it was. A rainbow! It must have fallen out of the sky and big pieces of it were blocking the creek so that the water couldn't flow on! The river beyond the fallen rainbow was just a slow trickle of water. So that's why they hadn't been getting enough water at the Angel Academy!

'I have to do something,' Ella said aloud to herself. 'But what?'

She raced down to the ground and looked at the broken rainbow. Close to, it was massive. She tried to drag one of the pieces off, but it was far too heavy and big. It didn't budge.

Ella wracked her brain. What could she do? Of course, she could go back and get help but then she would have to admit to being out beyond the school boundaries again and she'd probably lose ALL her halo points. It would be so much better

if she could just solve this problem on her own...

And then it came to her. Of course! *Maybe* she could make the rainbow disappear. She had seen Archangel Grace do it. She hadn't had a chance to practise but she might be able to do it!

She pulled her wand out and pointed it at the rainbow.

Rainbow please, now vanish away
Turn to glitter, do not stay.

Ella held her breath. Nothing happened. She pictured what Archangel Grace had done and suddenly gasped. Of course. She flicked her wand twice. The rainbow flashed with light and dissolved into glitter! She'd done it – the rainbow had gone!

With a whoosh and a splash, the water that had been backed up for so long came spilling down

into the empty river, overflowing the banks. Ella could hardly believe her eyes! There was water again! She'd saved the school's water supply.

She was just about to pat herself oven the back when a voice behind her made her startle.

'Ella!'

Ella looked up and her heart sank. Angel Gabriella was flying towards her. Someone must have told the teacher that Ella had flown away. Now she was really in for it.

Angel Gabriella landed beside her. 'I saw what you did from up there,' she cried breathlessly. 'Well done, Ella! You've got the water flowing properly again. It's amazing!'

'Really? You're not cross?' said Ella, feeling a wave of relief flood through her. She looked at the teacher cautiously. 'You do know I haven't got permission to be out here, don't you?'

Angel Gabriella laughed and gave Ella a massive hug. 'You're far too honest, Ella Brown, you know that? But honesty is an excellent angel quality. Of course I know you haven't permission to be out here on your own but if you hadn't been, the school's water supply would have run out completely!' she cried. 'Now come on... let's go and tell the others that you saved the day!'

☆ ☆ ☆

As Ella soared high up into the sky alongside Angel Gabriella she thought anxiously about what would happen. OK, so she hadn't been told off by her, but what would happen when Archangel Grace knew what she had done? She was sure that the head teacher wouldn't be so lenient. But there wasn't time to talk to Angel Gabriella about that now. It was all that Ella could do to keep up as they raced

through the sky. Soon, the glass castle of the Angel Academy was in their sights and Angel Gabriella started to slow down.

Ella flapped her wings and hovered mid-air. Lots of the other angels were still outside, practising for sports day. She could even see Archangel Grace supervising with the other teachers.

'Come on,' cried Angel Gabriella. 'Let's go and tell everyone the good news!'

'But Angel Gabriella,' said Ella. 'Aren't I going to be in trouble when we get there? I mean…'

'Leave that to me,' said Angel Gabriella.

Breathlessly they flew down to the ground.

'Angel Gabriella… Ella!' Archangel Grace fanned her face, 'You gave us quite a start coming down from the skies like that. Whatever is the matter?'

'We've got an announcement to make,' said

Angel Gabriella. She smiled at Ella. 'We've got water again! The school's water supply is back to normal. Sports day can go ahead!'

'What do you mean?' demanded Archangel Grace

'How was it fixed?' asked Angel Seraphina.

'What had been the problem?'

'What's Ella got to do with it?'

Excited questions filled the air as everyone gathered round. Archangel Grace held up her hand for silence.

'I think you'd better tell us more, Angel Gabriella,' said Archangel Grace looking serious.

'Ella?' said Angel Gabriella.

'It was a fallen rainbow,' Ella said breathlessly. 'Near the woods. It had fallen across the creek and broken into pieces. It was blocking the flow of water to the school.'

'You were over by the woods, Ella?' Archangel Grace said.

Archangel Gabriella stepped in quickly. 'Ella was the star of the day. She managed to turn the rainbow into glitter. I've no idea how she knew the spell.'

Archangel Grace gave Ella a shrewd look. 'Hmm, I wonder.'

Ella blushed.

'Well, however you knew, it's brilliant that you used the spell and saved the day!' Archangel Grace raised her hands skyward. 'We have water! This is cherubazing!' she cried. 'Sports day can go ahead after all! I shall go and tell the rest of the school!'

'With that, she disappeared off up the path.

Everyone started to talk excitedly. Ella's friends gathered round her.

‘I can’t believe you solved the water problem!’ Jess launched in.

‘And saved school sports day!’ said Tilly.

‘We’ll be able to have angel icicles again!’ cried Poppy.

Ella was delighted. Everything had happened so quickly. And it was so lovely that something as simple as lifting a rainbow and getting the water back to the school could have helped her make up with her friends.

‘We’ve got a surprise for you too,’ said Poppy, linking arms with Ella and leading her off.

‘A surprise?’ said Ella curiously.

‘Yes, come on,’ said Tilly.

Ella went with them excitedly. She liked surprises!

When they reached their dorm, Poppy, Jess and Tilly hung back.

'It's inside,' said Poppy.

Ella opened the door. And there, in the middle of the room, was the biggest, most scrumptious looking cake she had ever seen! It was hovering just above the floor and had layers and layers of chocolate and white icing. It was covered with silver stars and had a sugar sculpture of an angel on top.

'It's a CAKE!' she gasped.

'No, it's a squirrel!' joked Poppy.

'It's a special cake for you,' said Jess, taking her hand. 'We baked it.'

'Surprise!' Tilly and Poppy said in unison.

Ella stared at the amazing cake. 'So this is what's being going on over the last few days,' she realised. 'All the secrecy and whispering.'

'We wanted to cheer you up,' said Poppy.

Ella looked at her friends – from one to the

other. 'And you have,' she said. 'It's the best cake ever! Thank you!'

'Can we eat it now?' Poppy asked eagerly.

'Oh yes!' grinned Ella.

Over the next few days, the angels practised hard at their sports. On the night before the big event, hardly anyone could sleep! When they woke the next morning, the breeze had blown up and the temperature dropped slightly. It was the perfect weather for sports day.

In the afternoon, they all went to the sports field. All the parents and younger brothers and sisters had arrived. They were wandering round the field or sitting on the golden chairs lining the running track. The first years' first race was the sack race. When it was their turn, they went to the

start to line up with their silver sacks. Ella felt a little tingle of nerves run through her as she gazed at the crowds. Somewhere in the midst of it would be her mum and dad and little sister, Josie.

But there wasn't time to try and spot them. She would see them later on at teatime. Angel Gabriella raised her hand ready to start the race. As the flag fell, the first year angels were off, hopping madly forward. Jess was easily the sportiest of the four friends and took the lead quickly, closely followed by another angel called Holly, then Olivia Starfall sprung along behind. Tilly was mid-pack but Poppy and Ella were definitely nearer the rear of the field!

As Jess stretched through the winning line, Ella and Poppy tripped over each other and collapsed on the grass. They rolled over the finish line.

'What a race!' grinned Ella.

'Cool!' said Poppy. 'Well done, Jess!' she called as Jess went to collect her little red ribbon for first place.

'I've got to go,' said Tilly. 'I've got to be at golden archery in five minutes!'

Ella, Poppy and Jess gave in their sacks and

raced over to the other side of the field whilst Tilly joined the other archers at the pitch. She lined up, raised her bow and arrow... and struck the most perfect bullseye into the heart-shaped target.

'Way to go, Tilly!' Ella called out.

'What have you got next, Jess?' she turned brightly to her friend.

'Cloud hopping,' said Jess. 'And you?'

'I've got a little time-out in my schedule before the three-winged race,' said Ella. 'Poppy and I are doing that together.' She grinned at Poppy. 'Fancy getting a drink?'

'Angeltastic!' said Poppy and the two angels linked arms. 'Let's go and take a look around.'

Poppy and Ella headed off to the other side of the grounds to where the stalls of refreshments had been laid out. It looked very pretty – an area had been set aside for seating, and deck chairs and picnic rugs had been spread around. The whole of the school had been dressed with bunting – of cupids, and rainbows and stars and moons. Grabbing an angel icicle each from one of the stands, they mixed into the crowds. They had been wandering round for a while when the rainbow discus competitors started to get ready.

'Look, there's Primrose,' said Poppy, pointing out the angel who was standing with another group of angels in a roped off practice ring. The neat blonde angel had a look of concentration about her and her perfect features were scrunched up as she pulled her arm back and threw something up into the sky.

'Rainbow discus,' said Ella. 'They must be practising before the event. Come on, let's go and watch. I've got an idea which could be fun!'

While Ella and Poppy stood at the side, all the angels in the event lined up to take their practice turn.

'Out of the way, Veronica,' Primrose said,

rather bossily, pushing her friend aside as she stepped to the front. Taking a deep breath, she pulled her arm back and the piece of rainbow flew up into the sky... at exactly the same time that Ella pulled out her wand...

Ella pointed it at the rainbow discus and the discus started dispersing into the sky.

'Whatever's going–?' Primrose looked all about her, but just in time, Ella had put her wand away.

'Hmm.' Primrose shrugged, and grabbed herself another round piece of rainbow. She went to take aim. Again, Ella pointed her wand just as the discus went up into the air... and bounced out of Primrose's hand.

'Butter fingers, Primrose!' said her friend, Veronica.

'I didn't drop it, Vee,' Primrose hissed. 'Someone's playing tricks on me.' She looked

around, but Poppy and Ella were completely hidden behind a tree.

Primrose walked over to the discus, and went to pick it up again, so Ella waved her wand and sent the discus on a few paces. Again, Primrose went to pick it up but, just as she got a few paces away, the discus bounced away from her.

Poppy giggled. 'Stop it, Ella,' she said, creased over with laughter. 'It's too much.'

'But I've only just started,' Ella grinned mischievously.

Primrose, by now, was stopping and starting all over the pitch. Every time she got anywhere near the rainbow discus, it rolled on – just a few paces, but enough to make her completely exasperated.

'Is this you doing this, Veronica?' she hissed through gritted teeth.

'Of course it's not me, Primrose,' said Veronica, trying to hide her giggles.

'There, got it!' Finally Primrose had picked up the discus, but just as it was within her grasp, the disc slipped from her fingers and rolled off again.

'GAH!' cried Primrose. She looked so angry, steam was positively coming out of her ears! As she reached out to the discus, she gave it a large kick and it flung up into the air. Primrose lost her footing and fell over. She thumped the ground.

'Primrose!' a sharp voice called after her. 'What do you think you're doing?' It was Angel Raffaella. She helped Primrose up.

'Sorry, Angel Raffaella,' Primrose said humbly. 'It's this discus. It keeps on running away from me. I think someone must have put a spell on it.'

The discus lay flat upon the ground.

'It doesn't look as though it's moving to me,' said Angel Raffaella, going over to pick it up and hand it over to Primrose. 'See.'

'Oh...' Primrose looked embarrassed. 'Sorry, Angel Raffaella.'

'Hmm,' said Angel Raffaella, raising her eyebrows. 'Well, please try and keep your feelings under control. Now it's almost time for the event to start. Get ready please.'

She walked off – just as Ella and Poppy stepped out of the trees.

'Something wrong, Primrose?' asked Poppy.

'Is it you behind this, Ella Brown,' cried Primrose. 'Was it you making the discus move?'

'What discus?' said Ella innocently.

'MY discus,' shouted Primrose.

'Oh dear, Primrose,' said Ella, tutting and shaking her head. 'Are you shouting? Don't you remember that a good angel should never lose their temper? That's a direct quote from the angel handbook!'

'Oh, and angels should strive to be neat and tidy at all times,' said Poppy, brushing a spec of dirt off Primrose's collar. 'Isn't that something you are always reminding us about?'

'Grrrh!' cried Primrose.

But there wasn't time for her to retaliate as Angel Raffaella was just calling all the rainbow discus competitors into the ring.

'I'll get you for this, Ella Brown,' Primrose hissed. And, looking very red and angry, she stormed off into the ring.

8 The Prize-giving

As the competitors lined up behind the line, Ella and Poppy grinned at each other. 'Primrose looks in a bit of a tizz,' said Ella.

'Are you going to do the discus thing again, Ella?' said Poppy.

'No, not now it's the real competition,' said Ella. 'I don't think that would be fair. Primrose has had enough of a comeuppance for one day.'

As it turned out, Primrose wrecked her chances on her own. Instead of being able to laugh off what had happened in the practice ring, she was so cross, she stamped around the ring and threw the discus wildly. It went everywhere –

at one time even landing behind her!

Primrose stamped her foot, breaking the rainbow discus into two pieces. 'This CANNOT be happening to *ME*!'

'Primrose!' Angel Gabriella was shocked. 'Please will you leave the ring. No one wants to see such behaviour from an angel. I have to say I am very disappointed in you. I always thought you were such a good, well behaved angel.'

Primrose's parents were waiting for her. 'What is going on?' Primrose's mother looked just the same as her, only older, whereas Primrose's dad was somewhat plumper and had a superior look on his face. 'Whatever are you doing, darling?' they cried.

'I should have WON this event,' Primrose shouted.

'Of course you should, Primmy darling,' her

mother soothed. 'Come on, now let's take you off for a cherry icicle to cool you down.'

'I do NOT need a cherry icicle!' Primrose screamed.

Ella and Primrose caught each other's eye and snorted with laughter. 'Oh dear, poor Primrose,' said Ella.

'I don't think the teachers are going to believe she's perfect from now on,' said Poppy.

Ella watched Primrose go and shook her head.

'What is it, Ella?' said Poppy, seeing the change in her expression.

'Oh nothing,' said Ella. 'I'm just being silly, that's all.'

'If it's bothering you, it's not silly,' said Poppy.

'It's just even Primrose, who's the most horrible angel in our year, has got her sapphire

halo and… well, I haven't got mine. I'm the only angel in the year who hasn't made it to sapphire level yet.' She swallowed.

'Oh Ella,' said Poppy, giving her friend a hug. 'You'll get there. I know you will.'

'But when?' said Ella. 'It's not as though I'm going to be awarded anything for my sporting ability. And term is nearly at an end.'

'Well—' said Poppy, but she didn't have a chance to finish her sentence as an announcement was being made.

'Will everyone gather round please?' Archangel Grace called out loudly over a sparkly tannoy.

Poppy and Ella looked over and saw three blocks being laid out for prize giving.

'We've just finished our final event of the day – rainbow discus,' said Archangel Grace. 'So come

on over. It's time to collect your prizes!'

Poppy and Ella ran over and joined Tilly and Jess, who were standing in a group with their parents.

But now they were all called to hush as the first of the angels were being called up to collect their prizes. 'For halo hoopla,' called Archangel Grace. 'In third place, Olivia Starfall.' There was a loud cheer as a gentle looking angel with shoulder-length hair flew up to collect her medal. Everyone

clapped. 'In second place. Holly Willow.' Again, another round of applause and another medal. And in first place, Tilly Charming.'

'That's me,' Tilly beamed as she went up to collect the trophy – a golden angel perched on the top of a wooden plinth in mid-flight.

'And for golden archery...' the roll call went on. Through all the events – through rainbow discus, and the three legged flying race, through the silver sack race and the cloud hopping. There was even a prize for the angel with the perfect smile!

'And now,' Archangel Grace finished finally. 'We have a special prize to award.'

'A special prize?'

'What is it?'

Excited whispers filled the air as everyone looked from one to the other.

'This is for the angel who, in our opinion, has been the best sport throughout the day,' finished Archangel Grace

Who could it be? Excited whispers filled the air.

'Ella Brown, could you come up please?'

'Me?' Ella looked round her in surprise. 'Did she call me?'

'Well, I don't think there's another Ella Brown in the angel academy,' Poppy teased, gently pushing her friend up. 'Go on!'

Ella turned as red as a strawberry as she fluttered up to the podium to the sound of loud cheers and Archangel Grace handed her a trophy. Ella felt the best she had felt in ages, and the beam that stretched across her face, from cheek to cheek, showed it.

She was just about to fly off the podium

when Archangel Grace turned to her again. 'Not just yet, Ella,' she smiled. 'I've got something else for you. Have you got your halo card with you?'

'Well yes, but...' Ella was puzzled.

She pulled out the card and with five taps of her wand, Archangel Grace had filled it. Ella gasped. There on the card, were the final halo stamps that she had needed to go up to sapphire level. And now the card was glittering.

'Well done, my dear,' said Archangel Grace. 'Sports day wouldn't have been able to go ahead without you.'

Ella stood perfectly still as Archangel Grace tapped her wand to Ella's head and Ella's pearly white uniform turned to sparkling blue.

'Wow!' she cried as she looked down at herself. 'I love it! It's amazing!'

'Now, go on with you,' said Archangel Grace. 'And Ella?' she said softly.

Ella stopped on her way down from the podium. 'Yes?'

'You might not always be the perfect angel but no one deserves their sapphire halo more.' Her eyes met Ella's. 'I have high hopes for you, Ella Brown. Remember that.'

Ella felt a huge ball of happiness swell in her chest. She beamed and jumped off the podium. There was one group of people she wanted to see now – Jess, Tilly and Poppy – her very best friends. As she flew over to them, they surrounded her and gave her the biggest group hug.

'Didn't I tell you you'd do it?' said Jess.

'You look amazing,' said Poppy.

'I can't believe it!' cried Ella. 'I can't believe I've got to sapphire level. Perhaps I am a proper angel after all!'

'You're the most proper angel there is, Ella,' Poppy laughed. 'You're always saving the day.'

'Which is just what Guardian Angels have

to do,' said Jess.

For a moment Ella let herself imagine one day becoming a Guardian Angel with a diamond halo and beautiful big feathery wings. 'One day we'll all be Guardian Angels!' she declared

'But for now it's great just being us,' said Poppy.

Ella grinned. Poppy was right. They had so much fun together – and next year there would be even more adventures to come. 'We're so lucky!'

Jess lifted her wand and conjured a perfect rainbow that arched over the four of them.

Looking up at the sparkling colours, Ella spun round in delight. Being with her friends was the best place in the world to be. Her wings fluttered and she flew up. 'Bet you can't catch me!'

She set off into the sky with her friends chasing after her. Archangel Grace smiled as she

watched them. Behind her, the school's glass turrets sparkled in the rays of the summer sun.

The End

JOIN ELLA AND HER FRIENDS FOR THEIR VERY FIRST ANGELIC ADVENTURE IN THE SERIES,

New Friends

Angel Wings
New Friends
MICHELLE MISRA

'Oh, wow!' Ella Brown breathed as she looked through the big golden gates. On the other side of them was a castle made of pure glass. It sparkled like a diamond in the sunshine. Ella's wings fluttered. The Guardian Angel Academy.

It was just how she had always imagined it would be – totally perfect!

Ella checked her reflection in the shining gates. Her white halo was sitting straight, her brown, shoulder-length hair was glossy, and her green eyes sparkled. She couldn't wait to start her very first day!

She reached for the bell but, before she could press it, the gates swung open. A long driveway led to the castle entrance, parting fields of wild flowers. Bright butterflies flew from flower to flower and the gentle sound of bees hummed in the air.

Angel-tastic! This was going to be such fun! Ella half skipped and half flew forward, her tiny wings fluttering as they carried her along the drive. There were bound to be lots of adventures in store at angel school. She flew up and pirouetted at the thought.

'OK, so how *do* you do that?'

Ella spun round to see a very tall girl, about her own age, behind her. The girl was dressed in the same pearly-white uniform as Ella but she didn't look like your average neat and tidy angel. Her dress already had dirty splodges on it and a tangle of blonde curls were scrambling out from under her halo.

'Do what?' Ella asked, surprised.

'Make your wings work like that!' The girl peered over her shoulder at her own wings. 'I've been trying to make mine work ever since they appeared, but they just don't seem to. Look!' She jumped up in the air. Her wings gave a few faint flaps but didn't manage to lift her up. 'Oh, I'm useless!'

'No you're not. It just takes practice,'

Ella told her. I just think fluttery thoughts. Imagine you're a butterfly, swooping and gliding . . .' Ella was picturing it so clearly that her own wings fluttered and she rose into the air. 'Like that!'

she giggled, floating down again.

The tall girl concentrated hard. 'OK, here goes. I'm imagining, I'm imagining . . .'

'Keep on trying. You can do it!' Ella encouraged. The other girl's wings started to flutter faster and suddenly she shot up into the sky like a rocket.

'Whoa!' she cried in alarm, turning a loop-the-loop and coming down again, her arms flailing. She would have crashed to the ground but Ella rushed forward to catch her just in time.

'Thank you!' gasped the other girl. A grin lit up her face. 'Hey, I flew! I really flew! I might not have won any marks for style, but I did it – and it felt totally brilliant.' She hugged Ella, almost knocking her over. 'So what's your name? I'm Poppy.'

'I'm Ella,' Ella replied.

'And is it your first day too?' Poppy asked.

Ella nodded.

'Can we be friends?' Poppy said, giving her a hopeful look.

'Well . . .' Ella paused teasingly. 'Do you like adventures?'

'Oh yes!' breathed Poppy.

Ella broke into a smile. 'Then we can be *best* friends!'

Poppy grinned. 'That's totally *cherub-azing!*'

Ella linked arms with her and looked up at the glittering castle. 'Look out, Guardian Angel Academy. Here we come!'